4/2022

DISCARD

Mama and Mommy and Me in the Middle

Nina LaCour

illustrated by Kaylani Juanita

CANDLEWICK PRESS

MONDAY

The sun is still hiding and the moon is still bright
when Mommy kisses my cheek and says,
"Good morning."

Just like always, Mama takes down the plates,
I set out the napkins and forks,
and Mommy cooks the pancakes
until they are golden.

Mommy and Mama and me in the middle.
We eat until our bellies are full
and the sun has begun to warm the sky.

"I'll be home on Sunday,"
Mommy says, and then . . .
we wave goodbye.

At the café, when Jane calls my name,
two cups wait on the counter
instead of our usual three.

We sit and watch the neighborhood wake up.
I give myself a milk mustache and Mama laughs.

TUESDAY

During circle time I say, "My mommy is on a work trip."

Mr. Henry asks, "Is anyone else missing someone they love?"

Olive misses her sister, away at school.
They used to build block towers.

Miguel misses his papa, in a faraway country.
He wears a necklace to remember.

Chloe misses her cat
who ran away.

When it's dark out, Mama sets up the projector
and we watch a movie on the wall.
"Can we do this every night Mommy's gone?"
"Well . . ." Mama says. "Not every night."

WEDNESDAY

"Let's call Mommy," Mama says when I wake up.

"Yes!"

It rings and rings and then . . .

"My loves!" she says. "It's you!"

In the faraway place where Mommy is working,
snow falls from the sky.
Out the window of our house, rain pours down.
She tells me that rain is loud and snow is quiet
but both are made of water.

I squeeze shut my eyes and listen.

"I miss you as much as all the snow in Minnesota," she says.

"I miss you as much as all the rain in California."

"That's a lot of missing," she says.

I hug the phone and Mommy squeezes hers.

Then I give Mama a hug because real ones feel better.

At lunchtime, I sit on one side of Mama at the table.
Then I move to the other side.
It's tricky to find the right spot
when I'm not in the middle.

THURSDAY
It's errand day!
Library books—*thunk!*—into the slot.

Packages dropped at the post office.

I am always a big helper at the grocery store.

Apples for Mama. *Check!*

Blueberries for Mommy. *Check!*

Bananas for me. *Check!*

"But Mommy's still on her trip," Mama says.

"Oh," I say, remembering.

I put the blueberries back where I found them.

And later . . .

Gray sky. Mama's too busy to play.
Tears roll down my cheeks.

"Oh, kiddo. What's wrong?"

"I miss Mommy. I miss her as deep
as a scuba diver down in the ocean
and as high as an astronaut up in the stars."

"That's a lot of missing," Mama says.
"I miss Mommy, too. Let's snuggle up
and miss Mommy together."

Little by little, I feel better.

FRIDAY

Our walk to school is warm with sunshine
and speckled with puddles.
In front of one house, the flowers grow so big and wild
Mama and I have to walk single file down the sidewalk.

Here in the flower forest, I get an idea.
I whisper it to Mama.
"Yes," she whispers back.
"Keep it in your mind," I tell her.
"It's a plan," she tells me. "You don't forget, either."

COMMUNITY GARDEN

SATURDAY
I keep the plan in my mind as I help
Mama stuff our dirty clothes into the machine.
While I wash the windows with my own sponge
and water the plants on the windowsill.

While we color a welcome home banner for Mommy
and I build a city for my hedgehogs and pandas
and Mommy blows me a kiss from the phone and says,
"I'll see you tomorrow."

SUNDAY

A pair of scissors. A piece of string. A jar of water.
And off we go to the flower forest!

We snip lilies for Monday, the day Mommy left.
A poppy for Tuesday . . .
and yarrow for Wednesday.
Ferns for Thursday . . .
and foxgloves for Friday.
An aster for Saturday . . .

and a violet for today, Sunday, the day Mommy comes home.

The rain is gone and Mommy is coming home!
The puddles have dried up and Mommy is coming home!
The birds sing and Mommy . . .

IS HOME!

But then I remember . . .

Two cups instead of three, gray sky and tears,
and a carton of blueberries placed back on the shelf.
One whole week of missing.

I cover my cheek with my hand.
"It isn't a day for kisses," I tell her.

"I understand," Mommy says. "But I want you to know . . .
I missed you as deep as a scuba diver down in the ocean
and as high as an astronaut up in the sky."

"That's a lot of missing."

This time, when she opens her arms,
I snuggle in and Mama does, too.

It feels just right.

Mama and Mommy and me
in the middle.

For Juliet and her mama
NL

To my little sister, Melbie.
Even though you fall asleep during most movies and
play tricks on me, I miss you at the end of every visit.
You are the best at cooking and making everyone feel at home.
KJ

First edition 2022

Library of Congress Catalog Card Number 2021947060
ISBN 978-1-5362-1151-1

21 22 23 24 25 26 LGO 10 9 8 7 6 5 4 3 2 1

Printed in Vicenza, Italy

This book was typeset in Scala.
The illustrations were done in mixed media.

Candlewick Press
99 Dover Street
Somerville, Massachusetts 02144

www.candlewick.com